M000036423

BEFORE THE WERE FAMOUS

Babe Ruth

BEFORE THEY

Babe

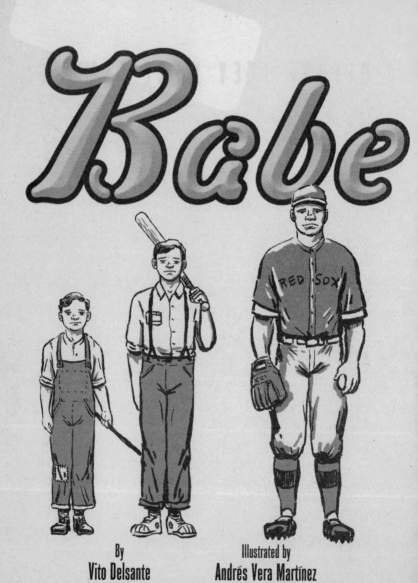

By
Vito Delsante

Illustrated by
Andrés Vera Martínez

WERE FAMOUS

Ruth

ALADDIN PAPERBACKS New York London Toronto Sydney

This book is a work of fiction. Any references to historical events, real people, or real locales are used fictitiously.
Other names, characters, places, and incidents are the product of the author's imagination, and any
resemblance to actual events or locales or persons, living or dead, is entirely coincidental.

ALADDIN PAPERBACKS
An imprint of Simon & Schuster Children's Publishing Division
1230 Avenue of the Americas, New York, NY 10020
Text copyright © 2009 by Vito Delsante
Illustrations copyright © 2009 by Andrés Vera Martínez
Adapted from Childhood of Famous Americans: *Babe Ruth* by Guernsey Van Riper Jr.
All rights reserved, including the right of reproduction in whole or in part in any form.
ALADDIN PAPERBACKS and related logo are registered trademarks of Simon & Schuster, Inc.
Designed by Christopher Grassi
Manufactured in the United States of America
First Aladdin Paperbacks edition February 2009
2 4 6 8 10 9 7 5 3 1
Library of Congress Control Number 2008929319
ISBN-13: 978-1-4169-5071-4
ISBN-10: 1-4169-5071-0

I dedicate this to my grandfathers, Vito and Emiliano,
who introduced me to baseball in the first place.

I'd like to acknowledge James Owen and Paul Crichton for getting me in touch with Liesa Abrams, a wonderful editor; Mike Lilly, who started this project; Andrés, who finished it and did more than I could ever have imagined with it; and finally Michelle, who is always an inspiration and muse.

—Vito Delsante

I dedicate this book and my work to my wife, Na; my daughter, Mei;
and the rest of my family who inspire me to live the life I love and
love the life I live.

I'd like to acknowledge my teachers from the School of Visual Arts: Marshall Arisman, Kim Ablondi, David Sandlin, Klaus Janson, Sal Almendola, and David Mazzucchelli. I'd also like to thank Brian Rea for seeing my potential and giving me my first break in the business; my agent, Bob Mecoy, for believing in my talent and introducing me to the fine editorial team of Liesa Abrams and Karin Paprocki; Vito, for writing such a charming story; and my interns, Ishmael Forde and Ricardo Blot, two high school kids with bright futures in art. They have all helped make the experience of working on this book easy, creatively fulfilling, and fun.

—Andrés Vera Martínez

GO AHEAD, GEORGIE!

BOOOM

C'MON, LET'S GET OUT OF HERE!

TRIP

SPLAT

UH-OH. IT'S MRS. CALLAHAN.

WHAT DOES *SHE* WANT?

KNOCK KNOCK

WAIT, JUST A—

WE'D BE HAPPY TO HEAR IT.

THERE'S A GOOD SCHOOL HERE IN BALTIMORE THAT MAY BE ABLE TO HELP GEORGE.

ST. MARY'S INDUSTRIAL SCHOOL FOR BOYS.

A CATHOLIC SCHOOL?

IT'S RUN BY THE BROTHERS OF THE XAVIERIAN ORDER. THEY DO GOOD WORK FOR BOYS IN DIFFERENT COUNTRIES.

HOW WOULD THAT HELP GEORGE?

HE COULD LIVE AT THE SCHOOL AND LEARN A TRADE. YOU'D NEVER HAVE TO WORRY ABOUT HIM SKIPPING CLASSES.

BUT THE BROTHERS WOULD BECOME HIS LEGAL GUARDIANS UNTIL HE TURNS TWENTY-ONE.

WHAT'S THE MATTER, GEORGIE? SURELY YOU COULD DO THAT FOR US, AFTER ALL THE TROUBLE YOU'VE CAUSED.

GEORGIE, YOU'RE NOT A BAD BOY. YOU'RE KIND AND GENEROUS AND FRIENDLY.

YOU CAN'T GO THROUGH LIFE WITHOUT SCHOOL, GEORGIE.

WHAT'S THAT, GEORGE?

I'D HAVE TO START OFF WITH ALL THE LITTLE KIDS?

WELL, THERE ARE SOME LITTLE FELLOWS . . . AND SOME FELLOWS YOUR SIZE. EVEN SOME BIGGER THAN YOU.

THEY'LL ALL BE AHEAD OF ME AND KNOW MORE THAN I DO.

WELL, YOU HAVE TO START SOMEWHERE, RIGHT?

LET ME GET THAT MITT.

HUH?

HEY! GEORGE! C'MERE!

C'MERE! WE'RE UP TO BAT!

THERE'RE NINE PLAYERS ON EACH SIDE, BUT IT REALLY COMES DOWN TO THE BATTER AND THE PITCHER

BASICALLY, THE PITCHER HAS THREE CHANCES TO RETIRE THE BATTER.

EVERY TIME THE BATTER MISSES A CHANCE, IT'S CALLED A STRIKE.

I HEARD BROTHER HERMAN SAY "BALL" A FEW TIMES. WHAT'S A BALL?

STRIKE!

DID'JA SEE THOSE TWO BOXES ON EITHER SIDE OF THE PLATE?

FAP

WOOOSH

YEAH.

A BALL IS A PITCH THAT COMES ACROSS EITHER OF THOSE TWO SPOTS. ANYTHING THAT COMES OVER HOMEPLATE IS IN THE STRIKE ZONE.

IF THE PITCHER THROWS FOUR BALLS, THE BATTER GETS A FREE BASE, CALLED A WALK.

SPAK

TO SCORE A RUN, A BATTER HAS TO TOUCH ALL FOUR BASES. PERCY JUST HIT A SINGLE, SO HE GOES TO FIRST BASE.

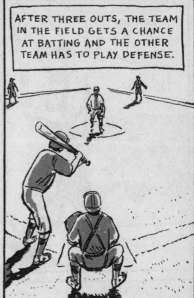

AFTER THREE OUTS, THE TEAM IN THE FIELD GETS A CHANCE AT BATTING AND THE OTHER TEAM HAS TO PLAY DEFENSE.

WOW! THAT KID JUST WALLOPED THE BALL!

KRAK

YEAH, BUT IT WENT OUTSIDE THE FOUL LINE. IT COUNTS AS A STRIKE.

GEEZ, THERE'S A LOT TO REMEMBER.

EH, DON'T WORRY. JUST HAVE FUN!

IT'S JUST A GAME!

GEORGE, YOU'RE UP TO BAT!

THERE GOES JOHNNY, ALL THE WAY OVER THERE.

OKAY BOYS, IT'S SEVEN-THIRTY.

I'LL BE BACK MOMENTARILY TO SAY GOOD NIGHT.

IT'LL BE LIKE THIS EVERY NIGHT FROM NOW ON.

SURE! I-I'LL STAY.

THAT'S GREAT!

BY THE WAY, I SHOULD LET YOU KNOW, I'M THE PREFECT OF DISCIPLINE.

DOES THAT MEAN I'M GOING TO GET PUNISHED?

WELL, WHY DON'T WE KEEP THIS BETWEEN THE TWO OF US. WHAT DO YOU THINK?

THAT'S GREAT THANKS!

BUT I DO EXPECT YOU TO FOLLOW THE RULES IN THE FUTURE. AND THE FIRST RULE IS THAT YOU SHOULD BE IN BED!

LATER . . . .

YOU GUYS WATCH! I'M GONNA HIT IT SO FAR. IT'LL—

GEORGE, I WANT YOU TO LAY DOWN A BUNT, OKAY? THIS WAY MARIO WILL BE IN SCORING POSITION.

GRUMBLE GRUMBLE BUNT! WHAT'S HE THINKING?! GRUMBLE GRUMBLE

HEY LOOK! GEORGIE THE SHIRTMAKER FINALLY MADE IT!

THAT'S ENOUGH, ROD.

BIP

I GOT IT! EASY OUT!

YOU SHOULD STICK TO SHIRT MAKING, GEORGIE!

WOW, GEORGE! YOU NEARLY TORE MY ARM OFF!

YOU THINK I DID GOOD?

GEORGE?

GREAT JOB, SON.

I TRIED TO TEACH YOU A LESSON AND YOU TAUGHT ME ONE INSTEAD!

SO WHAT DO YOU THINK?

I REALLY LIKE PITCHING!

WELL, FIRST, I THINK YOU OWE YOUR TEAMMATES SOMETHING.

SORRY ABOUT LAUGHING EARLIER, GUYS.

NO WORRIES, GEORGIE! YOU DID GREAT!

UNFORTUNATELY YOU'LL HAVE TO WAIT A FEW MORE YEARS, GEORGE, UNTIL YOU TURN TWENTY-ONE.

MY PARENTS ARE HAVING SUCH A HARD TIME.

I JUST THOUGHT... I JUST WANNA HELP THEM.

I MEAN, I'VE BECOME A PRETTY GOOD SHIRTMAKER, RIGHT, BROTHER MATTHIAS?

YES, YOU HAVE. ONE OF THE BEST.

THERE'S GOTTA BE SOMETHING I CAN DO.

A WEEK LATER . . . THE BIG GAME!

EXCUSE ME, BOYS. IS THAT SEAT TAKEN?

NAH, IT'S ALL YOURS, MISTER!

ARE YOU SOME KIND OF A REPORTER?

NO, I'M A BASEBALL TALENT SCOUT. NAME'S FARLEY.

WELL, WAIT'LL YOU SEE OUR FRIEND GEORGE RUTH! HE'S THE BEST!

SURE, KID. WHATEVER YOU SAY.

THAT WAS SOME GREAT PITCHING, GEORGE! FANTASTIC!

I DIDN'T LET MY FAMILY DOWN, DID I?

NO, SON, YOU CERTAINLY DIDN'T!

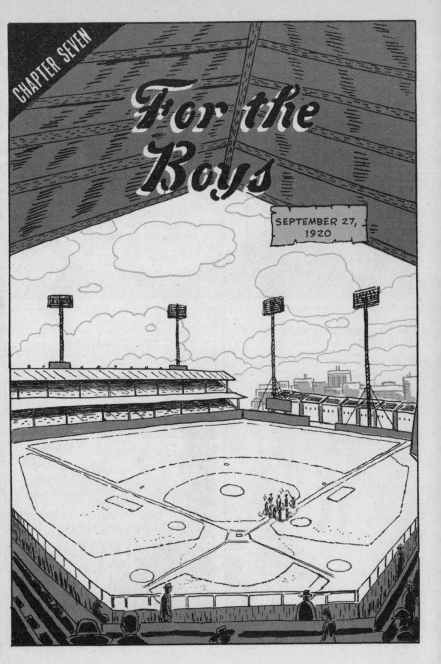

CHAPTER SEVEN

For the Boys

SEPTEMBER 27, 1920